PUFFIN BOOKS

Ian Whybrow is a bestselling author of over a hundred books who is proud to have been listed as one of the top ten most-read writers in UK libraries. Among his most popular characters are the hugely successful Harry and the Bucketful of Dinosaurs, the barking mad Sniff and the much-loved Little Wolf. Ian lives in London and Herefordshire.

www.harryandthedinosaurs.co.uk

Look out for more adventures with
Harry and the Dinosaurs:

ROAR TO THE RESCUE!

THE SNOW SMASHERS!

THE FLYING SAVE!

Harry and the Dinosaurs

A MONSTER SURPRISE!

Ian Whybrow

Illustrated by Pedro Penizzotto

PUFFIN

PUFFIN BOOKS

Published by the Penguin Group
Penguin Books Ltd, 80 Strand, London WC2R 0RL, England
Penguin Group (USA) Inc., 375 Hudson Street, New York, New York 10014, USA
Penguin Group (Canada), 90 Eglinton Avenue East, Suite 700, Toronto, Ontario, Canada M4P 2Y3
(a division of Pearson Penguin Canada Inc.)
Penguin Ireland, 25 St Stephen's Green, Dublin 2, Ireland (a division of Penguin Books Ltd)
Penguin Group (Australia), 250 Camberwell Road, Camberwell, Victoria 3124, Australia
(a division of Pearson Australia Group Pty Ltd)
Penguin Books India Pvt Ltd, 11 Community Centre, Panchsheel Park, New Delhi – 110 017, India
Penguin Group (NZ), 67 Apollo Drive, Rosedale, Auckland 0632, New Zealand
(a division of Pearson New Zealand Ltd)
Penguin Books (South Africa) (Pty) Ltd, 24 Sturdee Avenue, Rosebank, Johannesburg 2196, South Africa

Penguin Books Ltd, Registered Offices: 80 Strand, London WC2R 0RL, England

puffinbooks.com

First published 2011
2

Text copyright © Ian Whybrow, 2011
Cover illustration copyright © Adrian Reynolds, 2011
Text illustrations copyright © Puffin Books, 2011
Character concept copyright © Ian Whybrow and Adrian Reynolds, 2011
All rights reserved

The moral right of the author and illustrators has been asserted

Set in Baskerville
Printed in Great Britain by Clays Ltd, St Ives plc

British Library Cataloguing in Publication Data
A CIP catalogue record for this book is available from the British Library

ISBN: 978-0-141-33280-2

www.greenpenguin.co.uk

MIX
Paper from
responsible sources
FSC® C018179
www.fsc.org

Penguin Books is committed to a sustainable
future for our business, our readers and our
planet. This book is made from paper certified
by the Forest Stewardship Council.

This book is especially for Ted who is, as
he well knows, my absolutely favourite grandson.
And with grateful thanks, as ever, to the
Campbell family, my inspirational neighbours.

Chapter 1

Harry was up the top
of the old fir tree in the
garden, gasping for
breath. His hair was full
of pine needles and his
heart was pounding.

His sister, Sam, had gone
back into the house but
Harry had decided to wait
for a bit before he came
down. She was still mad

and might try to chase after him again.

While he was waiting to make sure the coast was clear, Harry thought about how he had ended up in the tree. It was like a scene from a soap opera!

Our Mad House

Episode nine zillion: 'The Blazing Row'

CAST (in order of speaking):

SAM: ~~My~~ Harry's horrible big sister. Pretty (I suppose). She thinks she is the BEST and that other people are

stupid. Spoilt and wants her own way all the time. Knows how to say nasty things to you in a clever way so you cannot answer back fast enough. Likes Wedge but also likes it when other boys tell her she is pretty.

WEDGE JENKINS: Sam's boyfriend. Tall. Works on his dad's farm so has big muscles. Handsome with interesting hairstyle. Funny and gets on with everybody. Likes machines, welding, cars, nature, going out, etc.

ME HARRY: Nice, popular, intelligent, likes adventure. Red hair. Belongs to special gang called the GOGOs with his friends Charlie, Jack and Siri. Also commander of a bunch of top-secret Back-Up Dinosaurs called B.U.Ds. These are not the little dinosaurs he used to carry about in a bucket when he was small. These are proper, scary dinosaurs!

SCENE: *The kitchen. Harry is halfway through a big bowl of Choxie Pops.*

    Enter Sam, in her nightie, yawning. Her mobile phone rings.

SAM: *(answering her phone)* Hi, Wedge. What's up?

WEDGE: All right, Sam? Listen, you'll never guess what I just bought at the car-boot sale. A couple of kayaks! Good as new. D'you fancy a paddle on the river tomorrow?

SAM: Kayaking? You must be joking! We're supposed to be going to a party tomorrow night, remember?

WEDGE: Yeah, but that's in the evening. There are some really good rare birds

nesting in the marshes at the moment. Come on, it'll be fun.

SAM: I'm doing my hair in the morning.

WEDGE: That won't take long, will it?

SAM: You can be so stupid sometimes, Wedge.

ME HARRY: Kayak? Tell Wedge me and the GOGOs will come!

SAM: (*to ~~me~~ Harry*) Will you be quiet, brat?
(*to Wedge*) I'll ruin my hair mucking about
in a boat!

WEDGE: Who are you telling to be quiet?

SAM: I'm not talking to you.

WEDGE: Oh right! Well, I'll go on my own
then!

ME HARRY: (*shouting*) We'll come, Wedge!
Take me and Siri and Jack and Charlie!

SAM: (*shouting at ~~me~~ Harry*) Go away!

WEDGE: You can be really mean, you can!

SAM: I'm not talking to you, stupid!

WEDGE: Who are you calling stupid?

SAM: Oh forget it!

*Sam hangs up on Wedge and goes into attack-
mode.*

Me Harry: *(running for it)* Mu-u-u-u-u-um!!!

THE END

After that, Harry spent quite a long time imagining the painful things Sam might do to him. It seemed wise to stay in the tree for a bit longer.

Harry reached into his pocket for his key-ring. He ran his fingers across the little plastic cards that dangled from it. They looked innocent enough – little flat dinosaur shapes, nothing more. But there was a reason why they were a closely guarded secret. They were his means of calling up a tribe of life-sized Back-Up Dinosaurs. If he was in serious trouble then

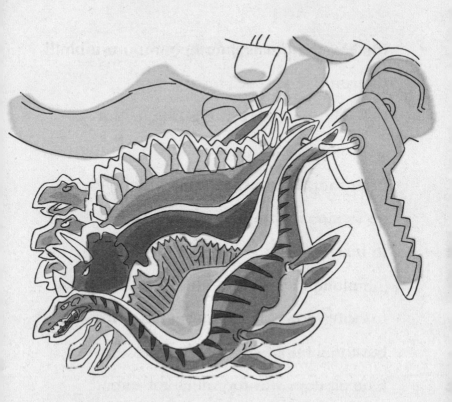

one of the dinosaur-shaped cards would
start to feel warm to the touch, meaning
that a B.U.D. was offering its help. He only
had to rub his thumb across the card in a
certain way and several tonnes of dinosaur
would be at his side and at his service! And

the best thing was that they were invisible to everyone except Harry.

Right now there was nothing. Not a spinosaurus, not a triceratops, not a raptor. Nothing. The cards felt cold and blank with no sign that anything interesting was about to turn up.

Finally Harry got so hungry he just had to climb down. It was not a smart move, but the thought of his half-eaten bowl of Choxie Pops was too much for him.

Unfortunately Sam knew it would be, too. She was waiting for him by the kitchen door like a cat at a mouse hole.

'Mu–u–u–u–u–m!!!'

Chapter 2

Later that day, when Harry had finally escaped from his sister, he headed to the secret meeting place of his gang, who had called themselves the Grand Order of the Great Oak. The other GOGOs – Charlie, Siri and Jack – sat scrunched up in the hollow inside the trunk of the Great Oak, their secret hideout in the woods. They were all deeply annoyed by Harry's story of his sister and the kayaks. The weather was sunny but the mood inside was dark and

gloomy. Nobody had a single cheerful thing
to say.

Charlie was fiddling with the ends of her
curly hair. Harry rubbed his thigh where
Sam had given him a dead-leg earlier.

Jack was fiddling with little bits of paper.

He nibbled them into wet lumps and flicked
them at people.

'Stop it, Jack!' grumbled Charlie. 'That's
disgusting.'

'What?' Jack replied angrily.

'Order, order!' said Siri, who liked

everyone to get on. 'If we can't go kayaking then we'll have to think of something else to do. Maybe we could ride our bikes over to Huntingdon?'

'Bo-ring!' said Jack.

'Harry, can't you speak to Sam and tell her to make up with Wedge?' asked Charlie.

'No way,' said Harry. 'I'm not begging her for anything. Anyway, she doesn't deserve him.'

Charlie crossed her arms in a sulk. Siri decided to change the subject. 'By the way,' he said cheerfully, 'did I tell you about my oldest cousin, Ravindra? He's got himself a job at last! He's a reporter for Heartlands TV.'

'TV! Wow!' exclaimed the rest of the GOGOs.

'It's good, isn't it? My aunty is so happy. Everyone always says he hasn't got the top brains of the rest of the family. But I like him. He phoned the house this morning to say that he's on the lookout for good local stories. Any suggestions?'

'You must be joking,' said Charlie. 'Nothing ever happens round here!'

'What about the rustling?' suggested Jack. 'The sheep and pigs going missing and all that.'

'It's not exactly big news, though, is it?' said Harry.

But Siri thought there might be something in it. 'You never know. It could be *really* exciting! Animals stolen for big money . . . criminal gangs from Europe, maybe . . . If we could track down these people, it could make an international story for Rav!'

Just then, Jack sprang up without warning and shot out through the overhead exit of the oak tree. He didn't say a word.

'Hey! Don't be like that,' called Charlie. She thought he was still annoyed about her getting angry with him earlier.

But Jack wasn't thinking about that. His smiling face looked down at them. He had hooked his legs over a branch and was

hanging down like
a little monkey.
'Come on, you lot,'
he said. 'Hurry up!'
Everyone
scrambled up and
out. Jack never
said much, but
it looked as
if he might
have a good
idea.

Chapter 3

THUNK. THUNK. KER-CHINGGG!

Wedge was flat on his back in the yard down at Jenkins Farm. Lying underneath his pick-up truck and hitting some hard lump of metal with a big hammer always made him feel better.

The first thing he saw of the GOGOs was the bottom of six bicycle wheels, four pairs of trainers and a skateboard. He couldn't see the dragon on the skateboard, but he knew by the colour it was Charlie's.

'What're you lot after?' he asked, not moving from under the truck. His old collie dog, Robot, came out and leaned on Harry, panting.

Here they were then. Jack's plan was simple. Pop over to Wedge's place, see if he needed cheering up. Maybe drop a few hints.

'We know you're not going to the river now . . .' said Charlie cautiously.

'And we understand why . . .' Siri said.

'But we just thought . . .' added Jack.

'You might like to show us the kayaks anyway?' Harry suggested.

'I bought life jackets and everything,' mumbled Wedge. 'And when I bought one kayak, the bloke threw the other one in free. Family-size, they are! Me and my dad used to have one when I was a kid. I've done safety courses and everything.'

'We have, too,' said Harry. 'At school.'

'Are they in the barn?' asked Charlie, peering around.

'Nope. They're in the back of the truck. Still folded, though. They need blowing up.'

'Ah, they're inflatables! Excellent!' Siri said enthusiastically.

'Yeah! They should be great actually!' said Wedge, catching Siri's good mood. He pulled himself out from under the truck, and grinned at the GOGOs. In a flash he was heaving the heavy green bundles out from the pick-up as Robot dashed around the barn barking with excitement.

Wedge set up the electric air pump. All it took was five minutes and there was the first kayak, blown-up and ready to go — bingo!

'What d'you reckon?' Wedge asked,

grinning from ear to ear. 'Luxury or what?'

'Brilliant!' chorused the GOGOs.

'You could easily get three people in that!' said Jack. He and Charlie were busy trying on safety-helmets while Siri had a go with a life jacket.

'Even my nervous mother would have to admit that this offers total protection for a

beginner like me!' he said eagerly.

'You'd be very safe!' Wedge agreed with a grin.

'Pity not to give them a go on the water,' said Jack casually.

'I was hoping Sam . . .' began Wedge, blushing a bit. He looked at Harry hopefully. 'Did she . . . say anything about changing her mind?'

Harry shook his head. 'Sorry, Wedge.'

'And did she say . . . Is she still going to the party tomorrow?'

Harry gave a shrug.

'Well, then,' Wedge sighed, giving his big hands a wipe-down on his overalls, 'we'll just have to launch these without her!'

Chapter 4

If Friday was a bright spring day, Saturday was *fabulous*. There was still no wind to speak of and not a cloud in the sky. Wedge and the GOGOs had an exciting ride to the River Midway.

Wedge had a really cool sound-system in his truck. Siri flicked through the radio channels and picked up the end of something on the news.

'. . . including special infra-red underwater cameras,' came an announcer's voice. 'While most experts agree that it's a waste of time and money trying to trace the Loch Ness Monster, Captain Simons and his team are determined to search the Scottish deep waters one more time.'

'Have you seen the photos in the papers?' asked Wedge. 'They're *obviously* fakes!'

'Mind you,' said Charlie. 'Imagine if this captain did manage to prove there was a monster!'

'What a sensation!' said Siri. 'I wonder,

ONCE MORE INTO THE DEEP!

is there a monster in the River Midway?
Ravindra would love to report on that for
Heartlands TV. It would make him famous,
I bet.'

'Probably make millions, too,' murmured
Jack. 'But there's no monster in the Midway.'

'I told my mum to let him know about
the sheep rustlers, though,' Siri said. 'Would

it be OK for Rav to go to the farm and have a word with your dad?' he asked Wedge.

'What, get on TV?' said Wedge. 'My dad would love that!'

'I'm going to call him now, then.' Siri pulled out his mobile and called his cousin. 'Don't forget to mention Wedge's name,' he said as he finished talking to Rav.

'Ask him if he wants to come over and film us looking for rare birds!' said Charlie.

Siri spoke to Rav some more, and then hung up. 'He said he's going over to the farm with a camera crew now, Wedge. And sends us good luck for the birdwatching but he's got to follow this story first.'

The gang was disappointed not to get a

chance to be on TV but then a good song
came on the radio and cheered them up.
Even Wedge, who was still upset about Sam
and the party.

'I've thought about how to solve your problem with Sam, too,' said Harry. 'Just be a bit bossier with her!'

Charlie rolled her eyes and shook her head. 'Sometimes you just don't understand girls, Harry,' she said.

Wedge squirmed in his seat. 'It's my fault really. I should've realized she just wants to look extra-nice for the party and everything. Me, I'm just a scruff-bag . . .' He fizzled out, looking miserable again.

'You'll be all right!' said Charlie. 'She'll get over it.' She gave Harry an elbow in the ribs for reminding Wedge in the first place.

Luckily that was just a little blip in what was otherwise a fun ride. There were cold drinks in the icebox and a jumbo packet of chocolates in the glove compartment.

'This is going to be so much fun!' said Jack.

Everybody felt happy and nobody even *thought* of asking if they were nearly there yet.

Chapter 5

When they arrived, Wedge drove up a dusty track that led to a slipway down into the river.

'Which way's the sea?' asked Harry, and Wedge pointed to their right.

The only other vehicle in sight was a van with an extendable ladder on the roof-rack. They pulled up in a cloud of dust next to it, and a skinny middle-aged man in camouflage clothing gave them a nasty look. He was disconnecting a trailer from the back of his van. On the trailer was an orange inflatable powerboat with a big motor.

'Hi there,' said Wedge cheerily. 'You off looking for birds, too?'

'Fishing,' grunted the man, scowling and making a big thing about fanning the dusty air away from his miserable face.

'Sorry about the dust,' said Wedge. 'I didn't realize the track was that dry! Can we give you a hand getting your boat in the water?'

The scowl on the man's face turned to something nastier as he made it clear he didn't want any help. He seemed determined to struggle with the boat on his own, even though it was loaded with lots of gear. Wedge shrugged his shoulders and got on with getting the kayaks down from his truck.

When the powerboat was in the water, Wedge made another attempt at a friendly question. 'Don't suppose you've seen any good birds since you got here, have you? I heard tell not long ago they've had peregrine falcons here. There was even a whisper about a pair of marsh harriers. You haven't . . .'

'Not interested, son,' said the man. 'Fishing is my thing.' He pointed in the opposite direction from the one he was taking. 'If you want birds – try over in that direction. *Way* over in that direction.'

Everyone turned to look inland and saw mudflats criss-crossed with shallow, oozing channels. They didn't look at all inviting. The only living thing to be seen was a man

in a rowing boat. Jack raised his binoculars
to get a better look.

'That doesn't look like a place where
birds would live,' said Siri.

Harry laughed. 'But a monster might –
the River Midway Monster!'

His voice was drowned out as the
powerboat's engine started with a roar.
Then the man headed off in the direction
of the sea. His boat quickly got up speed,

leaving two waves in its wake that bashed
against the shore and made everything
sway and bob. Water smashed up against
the ramp and surprised everyone, soaking
their socks and trainers.

'Eeek!' shrieked Charlie. 'I bet he did that
on purpose!'

Chapter 6

With Wedge to instruct them, the GOGOs
were soon on the water and paddling the
kayaks. Wedge had Siri and Charlie in with
him and Harry and Jack took the other
boat. Jack might look slight and skinny,
but he was strong and, like Harry, he had
been kayaking before. The two boys made
a good team, working together and calling
out to each other to change direction or
slow down.

There was a lot to learn but Siri and

Charlie were clever and soon got the hang of it. After about half an hour of practice near to the riverbank, Wedge declared that everybody was safe to push on downstream and explore.

'Let's go, maties, har-har!' called Wedge in his pirate voice and off they went.

Wedge made Charlie and Siri do most of the paddling while he steered and got ready to take plenty of photos.

'Nice camera!' puffed Siri.

'Here,' panted Charlie. 'Aren't we going the wrong way? That man in the powerboat said the birds were over the other way.'

'Well, he was wrong. There's no

protection for most birds to make nests down on the mudflats,' said Wedge. 'There are plenty of waders but not the birds we want to see. That bloke was just trying to get rid of us. Come on, we'll just take the main channel in the same direction he was going. We'll head for that tall tree, look . . .' He pointed. 'Then we'll take a left and explore one or two side-creeks.'

Everybody soon forgot about the strange man as they worked their way downstream. With a slack tide and very little breeze, they made good progress and soon they found themselves surrounded by rich vegetation.

They learned to make quiet strokes and to keep their conversation to a whisper as they floated through narrower and

narrower gaps between the reed beds.

That way, they didn't miss the water voles

crossing in front of them, or the frogs that

sat belching on lily pads or that leapt

gracefully into the water.

After a while, they came to a low island

and beached the kayaks where the mud

was not too slick.

'I used to come here with my dad,'
whispered Wedge. 'This is ideal for raptors.'

The hairs on the back of Harry's neck
started to rise. *Raptors*.

'Raptors meaning *dinosaurs*?' Siri asked.

'No!' laughed Wedge. 'Raptors meaning
birds of prey.'

Harry relaxed and laughed along with

the rest of the GOGOs. Why couldn't he keep dinosaurs out of his mind? His B.U.Ds key-ring was safely in his pocket, and there was no reason to call on their help today.

'Let's go ashore here,' said Wedge. 'It's an island. You lot follow me. Keep to the path and bring your bins.'

'He means binoculars,' Charlie whispered to Siri.

'I *know*!' hissed Siri. 'I didn't think we were going to collect litter!'

They dragged the kayaks ashore and left them in a safe place away from the water. The reeds grew tall on either side of the narrow, sandy track. Charlie was making a note on a little pad she carried and Wedge was snapping away with his camera every time he saw a bird.

Suddenly Wedge stopped. He lifted his binoculars towards the tops of a group of willow trees on the other shore of the small island. 'There!' he said in a hushed voice. 'Look at that! A pair of 'em! Definitely marsh harriers. See the black wing-tips? *Must* get a shot of them! There can't be more than three or four hundred pairs in the whole country!'

The GOGOs lifted their binoculars and watched the graceful creatures wheeling and diving.

'They look like they've been disturbed,' muttered Wedge. 'The female is flying about but she should be keeping her eggs cosy and warm. I wonder what's upset them?'

At that moment, they were all startled by a sudden noise that cut through the quiet morning like a chainsaw. It was the growl of a powerful engine starting up, and it was coming from over near the willow trees.

Chapter 7

Wedge was worried. 'Come on!' he said. 'Let's get along by the shore and see what we can find. Hurry up!'

They all took off towards the willows in double-quick time, towards the growling sound of the motorboat that was moving along the shore out of sight on the other side of the island. They knew that it would have to move slowly, especially with the narrowness of the creeks and the danger of going aground in the shallow water.

Overhead the birds were still streaking around, making their nervous screaming cries.

'What are we looking for?' asked Harry.

'We're looking for a big nest among the reeds. If I remember rightly,' said Wedge, 'marsh harriers build their nests quite close to the shore. Normally the public can't go near them at breeding-time. And fishing is *definitely* not allowed. So something tells me this is an emergency!'

'Stop!' came a loud voice. There were hurrying footsteps behind them. 'What on earth do you think you're up to?' A young man, not much older than Wedge, was moving fast along the path towards them. He had wind-burnt cheeks and was wearing shower-proof trousers with a

padded waistcoat and a wide-brimmed hat.
Slung over one shoulder was a rucksack,
and he carried a powerful-looking
birdwatching telescope on a tripod.

'This is a protected area,' he panted.
'You're breaking the law!' Suddenly he gave
a cry and fell heavily. He tried to get up but
couldn't.

Wedge pushed past the others to get back to him and saw that the young man's face had gone very pale. 'You all right, mate?' he said gently.

'I got my tripod caught on something and tripped over it. Blast! I think I might have busted my ankle. Arrgggh! That's painful.'

Wedge told him to lie still and had a look at his ankle. 'That's nasty,' he said. 'We'll have to get you to hospital. Are you a warden on the reserve here?'

The man nodded, holding his breath. 'Mike Lines, deputy warden. Didn't you see Brian, my boss?' he asked through gritted teeth. 'He's on patrol, too. He must have told you to keep well away from here, surely?'

'Sorry, we haven't seen anybody around

here,' said Harry. *Including you until now*, he thought. But then he realized that a warden would have to know the river and creeks very well, and he'd be taking short-cuts.

'But we did *hear* someone. Listen,' added Charlie, putting her finger to her lips. The engine-sound was growing faint but it was still there.

'That's a worry,' said the man, wincing with pain. 'Brian's only got a rowing boat so he doesn't disturb the birds. So that's not him.'

'Was Brian in a grey boat with green trim?' asked Jack. And when the warden nodded, Jack told him that they'd last seen

it heading for the mudflats.

'Well spotted!' said Charlie.

'And I bet I recognize that motor,

too,' said Wedge. 'Sorry, mate. Looks like your boss, Brian, has been tricked. And we know who by – because a bloke in a powerboat tried to do the same to us!' He patted Mike on the shoulder. 'Before we shift you, you'd better let us know where that harrier nest is. And quick!'

Mike explained as best he could and then he and Wedge worked out a complete plan of action. First, Wedge and Harry would go and check the nest and the others would stay with Mike and keep him warm and comfortable. Wedge and the GOGOs had all left their mobiles locked in the truck, not wanting to risk getting them wet, so Mike would have to use his phone to call an ambulance and ask for it to meet them at the truck. Then he'd have to call up Brian and let him know what was happening.

Harry bustled along the path after Wedge. When they reached the willows, not far from where the harriers were gliding, they approached boggier ground where the reeds grew thicker. They had to stoop as they walked, gently spreading apart bunches of reeds with their hands. They were lucky.

'Here!' Harry said, and Wedge was at his side in a few seconds, looking down at the tangled, shallow structure of the bird's nest. It was empty.

Wedge put the flat of his hand on it. 'Still warm,' he said. 'I bet there were eggs in there till just a few minutes ago.'

'Well, we've got a pretty good idea who's got them, haven't we?' said Harry angrily. 'Mister Misery in the orange powerboat.'

'Well, he's got away with it,' said Wedge with a sigh. 'We ain't got a hope of catching him. He could easily be back at his van by now – and we've got to get Mike out of here.'

Without thinking, Harry's hand went to his pocket and felt for the plastic cards on his key-ring. One of them was as warm as toast!

I might just have a plan, he thought to himself. *A Back-Up plan!*

Chapter 8

There was more bad news when they got back to the others. Mike hadn't been able to contact Brian. Either his phone was off or there was no signal wherever he was. But at least they'd managed to get through to the ambulance by calling 999.

'Listen up, guys,' said Wedge, and he got things organized. Everyone would help carry Mike back to the boats. It was too awkward for the warden to wriggle into his one-man kayak, so Harry would have to paddle it. Meanwhile, Mike could stretch out in one of Wedge's inflatables and paddle as much as he could, with Siri on board to steer; and Wedge, Charlie and Jack would tow them from the other three-seater.

'I'd better go ahead,' said Harry. 'You lot will have to paddle pretty slowly and somebody should be around to meet the ambulance. And maybe I can find Brian and let him know what's happening.'

'Be careful, Harry,' said Wedge. 'I'm only letting you go alone because it's an emergency.'

'I'll be safe,' he promised, thinking about the key-ring that was warming his pocket.

While Harry put on his safety gear, Mike told him the quickest route back to the main channel. 'It'll be a while before the tide turns, so it'll be hard going – but it shouldn't be too bad,' he said.

Harry was soon sliding into Mike's kayak and adjusting everything to fit him. Then he carefully pulled his key-ring out of his pocket and slipped it on to his finger so he could grip it and paddle at the same time. The others gave him the thumbs-up and Wedge pushed him into the water.

Off Harry went along the
narrow ribbon of water; his steering
was a bit zig-zaggy at first. Once

or twice he jammed the front of the
kayak into the reeds and had to

back up but soon he learned how
to stay in a straight line. It wasn't
long before he was out of sight of
the others and had reached the
edge of the reed beds. The nose
of the kayak was in the main
channel and he could feel the
current tugging him towards the
sea. He reached out with one hand

and grabbed a handful of rushes to hold the kayak still.

Then he laid the paddle across his lap and felt through the tiny collection of plastic cards dangling from the key-ring. The third one felt warm enough to be on stand-by. The shape was getting brighter but there was no time to work out which dinosaur it was. The first time a life-sized spinosaurus had appeared in his bedroom, it had explained that the cards would only work if Harry rubbed them in the right direction. Now, he carefully ran his finger along the edge of the card, making sure that he stroked the creature *nose-to-tail*.

WHAM!

Chapter 9

Harry found himself face to face with the flat greenish snout and wide-open jaws of a beast with a very scary set of teeth! They were razor-sharp, like cone-shaped spears, overlapping top and bottom. Harry gulped.

'Y-you must be . . .' stammered Harry.

'Plesiosaurus dolichodeirus, at your service,' said the creature, but not in the sort of voice that sounded at all keen to serve Harry. 'Oh. Wait!' It suddenly dipped its surprisingly short, slender head into the water and came up with enough dangling weed to build a small green haystack. No sooner

had the head re-
emerged than it rose
up from the water on
a neck longer than the
kayak. The creature's
neck looked a bit like
a palm tree, bending
slightly and with dark
hoops round it every
twenty-five centimetres
or so. With a violent
flick that sent Harry
rocking like mad in the
kayak, the beast tossed
the weed aside and at
the same time flipped a
couple of large fish into

the air. They dropped into the dark cave of its mouth with a *slop* and a *gloop*.

'Now, listen,' said Plesiosaurus. He sounded as if he was used to getting his own way. 'You're in a hurry, right? OK. I need a rope around my tail. How are your knots? Can you manage a clove hitch?'

'A c-clove hitch . . . um . . . I think so,' said Harry, not quite sure if this was really happening. With a big effort, he gathered the tow-rope that Mike had neatly stowed and twisted the end into two loose overlapping loops, ready to be attached.

Plesiosaurus rolled his smooth body in the water like an otter and two pairs of huge flippers appeared. He clapped them together with cracks like double pistol-shots! The dinosaur was at least five metres long – about the length of Mister Misery's van and trailer from nose to tail. When he rolled upright, Harry could see that his body was as bulky as an elephant's, only longer. He also noticed that as Plesiosaurus moved out into the centre of the channel, where the water was brown, the colour of the dinosaur's skin was changing.

'How do you do that?' asked Harry with a gasp.

'What, change colour? I'm adaptable –
that's it, end of story.'

'I can see that,' said Harry. 'Now, could
we . . . ?'

'Hurry up with that tow-rope!'
interrupted Plesiosaurus in a bad-tempered
voice.

Harry dropped the hitch over the tail
that was aimed towards him and pulled the
knot tight as quickly as he could.

'Right!' said the dinosaur. 'Let's crunch

arms and legs!' With that he started to paddle downstream.

Harry decided things were getting a little out of hand.

'Hey, look here,' he said, trying to sound firm. 'I haven't even told you where we're going yet! First, I'd like to catch up with a man in an orange inflatable dinghy with a motor. He's heading for a ramp about two

miles *upstream*. He's got a van with a trailer parked there.'

'Listen, do you think I can't read your mind?' said the bad-tempered creature. 'I know *exactly* who you're after. And I'm telling you he's heading towards the coast. Right, do you want to catch up with him or not? I can rip off his head, if you want . . .'

Harry took a deep breath. 'Now, you listen to *me*!' he said, in his most serious voice. '*You* are supposed to be at *my* service; you said so yourself.'

'Yeah, well . . .'

'So we do things my way. I'm in charge,' snapped Harry.

Plesiosaurus whacked the water with a front flipper and let out a bellowing

roar that thundered over the marshes and
sent hundreds of water birds flapping and
splashing away in a panic.

Harry had to struggle to settle the kayak
that was rocking again like a wild horse.
That's why it took him a moment to realize
that he had just heard the sound of a
marine dinosaur laughing.

Chapter 10

At first, Harry was unsure what to do.
Plesiosaurus was whining and straining
at the rope like a pack of huskies. Should
he command the creature to take him
back upstream to meet the ambulance?
Or should he go after the powerboat that
the dinosaur said had gone the other way?
Finally he decided that the ambulance
would take a while to arrive and that it
would have to wait for the injured warden
to turn up anyway. So he braced himself

and shouted, 'OK, downstream!'

'Whatever you say. You're the chief,'
said the more obedient beast, and plunged
forward.

The dinosaur swam like a giant dolphin,
its long body looping in and out of the
water. It raised its front end above the
surface, stretched out its fore-paddles,

ducked its neck and body underwater, then followed through with its rear-paddles.

All Harry could do as Plesiosaurus gathered speed was to hang on for dear life. And now and then he had to steer his kayak back into the creature's slipstream and away from the waves that followed. He had taken plenty of boat rides before – but they had been nothing like this! They were soon cutting through the water like a turbo-charged lifeboat.

After a short while, the narrow channel opened up and they left the reed marsh far behind. Harry soon found himself gazing up at tall chalk cliffs, and in the distance he could make out houses and hotels. He suddenly realized that they had reached the point where the river joined the sea and he

was looking up towards the seaside town of

Eastbrook.

They were passing a sheltered cove
when Harry spotted a flash of orange.
The powerboat! he thought. At that moment,
Plesiosaurus stopped paddling and allowed
the kayak to swing in a thrilling arc before
coming to a stop. So it was true what the
dinosaur had said about being able to read
Harry's mind. Still, Harry didn't want to
take any chances. 'Move along to the next
cove. I want to keep out of sight,' he ordered.

'Aye-aye, captain,' answered his personal
tug-boat in a strange bubbling voice. Harry
still didn't really know how far he could
trust Plesiosaurus. Was the dinosaur joking
with him or was he being serious? Anyway,
he did what he was told and pulled Harry
in towards the cliff.

Looking up, Harry
suddenly noticed a rope
dangling from just below
the top of the cliff. As he
got closer, he could see
that the rope hung all the
way down to where the
powerboat was moored.
And there was the man
in the camouflage vest
and trousers! Mister
Misery was way up the
cliff, suspended on the
rope, reaching out over

a ledge. He found
something and
carefully placed it behind
him into one of a number
of small pouches hanging
from a strap around his
middle. He reached out
again, and once more
put something into a
pouch.

Two angry birds,
jet black with long red
beaks, attacked the
climber like mini jet
planes. He was forced
to raise an arm and
flap his baseball cap at

them. At once he pushed off with both feet and abseiled down the rope like he was in an action movie.

By now, Harry was tucked well into the neighbouring cove. Minutes later he heard the engine of the powerboat starting up. He ducked behind a rock. Plesiosaurus took the hint and disappeared below the surface of the water like a submarine.

Next thing they knew, the powerboat was cutting its way back down the estuary. Mister Misery had put on a navy blue sweater over his camouflage vest. Suddenly he looked like just any ordinary, innocent bloke on a fishing trip.

Chapter 11

The powerboat had set off at a cracking
pace, sending up a shower of spray behind
it. Harry was close behind but had kept a

bit of a distance because, in the excitement of the chase, he had forgotten that Plesiosaurus was plain as day to *him* but invisible to everybody else. A kayak going at top speed would look very odd if Mister Misery turned around!

When the plastic cards had first appeared on his key-ring, Spinosaurus had explained to Harry that he could make dinosaurs appear in any size he wanted. They would be solid but leave no footprints. They could be heard and smelled and touched, but never seen unless Harry gave the command.

When the powerboat reached the channel through the reed beds, it finally began to slow. Altogether, it had taken no more than ten minutes to reach the

place where the van was parked alongside
Wedge's truck.

As Mister Misery turned off his engine
and let the powerboat drift towards the
slipway, an ambulance appeared. Blue
lights flashed through a cloud of dust by
the water. Harry saw the driver lower his
window to have a word with a man in a
grey rowing boat with green trim.

That must be Mike's boss, Brian the bird-warden! thought Harry.

Mister Misery looked flustered for a moment and he spun round, as if looking for somewhere to escape to. That was when he caught sight of Harry bobbing downriver in the kayak. A cunning smile appeared on the man's face. For some strange reason, he looked delighted to see Harry. He cut his engine, stooped and looped a rope over a mooring bollard by the slipway. He brought his boat to a smooth stop just below his waiting van.

The bird-warden spotted Mister Misery and rowed within hailing distance, shouting, 'Hey! You told me there was a gang of vandals out on the mudflats doing damage!

But there's no one there!'

Mister Misery was positively friendly.

'Oh, hello again,' he said, actually smiling.

'Didn't you catch any of the little monsters?
They were chucking stones at a bunch of
curlews when I saw them. I told them off
but they took no notice of me.'

'So you said,' panted Brian. 'Well, I rowed all the way down to Dutchman's Creek but I didn't see hide nor hair of any kids disturbing birds.'

'Sneaky young things, eh?' said the man. Then he turned round. 'But look! There's one of them now – bold as brass!' He pointed at Harry.

Brian turned and saw Harry. 'And that's Mike Lines' kayak!' he shouted. 'He must have pinched it! Grab him!'

'Did you say Mike Lines?' yelled one of the paramedics, who had jumped down from the ambulance. 'That's the name of the casualty we're looking for!'

Mister Misery drowned him out by revving up his boat's engine with a roar,

and moving away from the slipway.
This was all too much for bad-tempered
Plesiosaurus. He plunged forward, and with
a growling snort he sank his teeth into the
body of the powerboat and shook the life
out of it.

BLAM!

The engine exploded with
a bang that made everyone
crouch and cover their ears.
Mister Misery was thrown
high into the air. He came
down with a howling
scream and hit the water
with an almighty splash.

It was a good thing Harry kept his head — otherwise Mister Misery wouldn't have kept *his*. As he came up spluttering out of the shallow water, Plesiosaurus opened his monster jaws and got ready to bite the man's head off. But Harry's thumb moved quickly over the little card on his key-ring *tail-to-nose*, the reverse of what he'd done before. Like a puff of steam, the monster evaporated, leaving Mister Misery in the water and the warden bobbing about in his boat in the wild waves Plesiosaurus had stirred up.

'What was that?' exclaimed one of the paramedics, as they both rushed down the slipway to help.

'Was it the engine? Or a gas canister, maybe?' yelled Brian. He had jumped out of his boat and was wading through the chest-deep water towards Mister Misery. 'Help me get him out, quick! He's knocked the wind out of himself!'

Together the three men pulled him out of the river and laid him gently on the bank. They were careful to support his head and to place him in the recovery position. 'Let's get his wet jumper off,' said one of the paramedics. 'We'll get a warm blanket on him.'

That was how they uncovered the strap around his middle and the pouches.

'Good grief!' exclaimed Brian. 'These are socks filled with packing of some kind, and ...' He put his hand inside one and felt around.

'Ahoy there!' came the excited voices of

Jack and Charlie. They had made excellent
time towing Siri and the injured Mike Lines,
thanks to the mighty muscles of Wedge.

'What are those, then?' asked the
ambulance driver. The warden was holding
up an egg in each hand for him to look at.

'This one's a marsh harrier's egg – and
this one, if I'm not mistaken, belongs to
a red-billed chough! We've got the only

breeding pair outside Wales and Scotland. They're nesting on the cliffs down towards Eastbrook right now. This is unbelievable! Their nesting site was supposed to be top secret.' The warden looked down at Mister Misery, who was coming to, looking dazed and moaning to himself. 'I think I'd better call the police right now!'

Chapter 12

Wedge, the GOGOs and Brian the bird-warden were all gathered on the riverbank. The ambulance had long gone and the police car had followed close behind. Mike Lines was on his way to hospital and Mister Misery – real name James Staples, egg-thief – was on his way to the local police station.

'Very well done, you guys!' the bird-warden was saying. 'You did an excellent job with poor old Mike. And boy, am I glad that we caught that man red-handed. What

a bit of luck that his boat went bang! I still
haven't got a clue how it happened.'

'Just as well,' Harry mumbled to himself.
I would have had a bit too much explaining to do!

Everyone looked at the crates stacked in
the back of the van. They were packed with
cotton wool and neatly lined with hundreds

of eggs – all in different shapes and sizes and colours!

'That's what they're like, these egg-stealers,' the warden explained. 'They get hooked on collecting. The man who stole these has probably been trying to get an egg from every species of bird in the country. The police say he's already got a record for this sort of thing.'

Siri snapped his fingers in frustration. 'This is a big story!' he said with a groan. 'Rav should be here getting this on camera!'

'Well, he can't be in two places at once,'
Jack pointed out.

'Now, if you'll excuse me . . .' said Brian.
He explained that he had to go because
the police had asked him to drive the van
and trailer over to the police station. They
needed them as evidence. He shook hands
with Wedge and all the children, inviting
them to come back for a private guided tour
of the bird sanctuary any time they liked.

'I wonder what happened to the
powerboat,' said Charlie as they all watched
the trailer disappear with the flattened
wreck of the orange dinghy strapped to it.

'Yeah, that was weird,' said Jack. 'Any
ideas, Harry? You must have been pretty
close when it blew up.'

'Er, well, it just sort of . . . happened,' stammered Harry. 'It must have been something to do with that big motor.' And then, to change the subject, he added quickly, 'Shouldn't we load up now?'

'Look at the time!' gasped Wedge, checking his watch. 'I need to get home and changed for the party. I mean, just in case . . . you know . . .' He couldn't quite bring himself to add that he was hoping Sam would forget their argument and go with him. 'Heave-ho, you lot!' he said.

They were checking the ropes that secured the two kayaks to the roof of the truck when a car with the words HEARTLANDS TELEVISION printed all over it arrived.

'Oh no!' wailed Siri. 'It's Rav! And he's missed all the excitement!'

As he spoke, a very smart-looking Sri Lankan man in his early twenties stepped out on to the dusty track. There was no mistaking who he was. He had exactly the same broad, bright smile as Siri. He said hi to everyone and introduced his cameraman, Ron.

'What are you doing here?' asked Siri.

'Didn't you have any luck with the rustlers?' asked Wedge.

Rav shook his head. 'It was all over by the time we got to Jenkins Farm. Your dad had got a message that a butcher from Stapleton was organizing the thefts from farms all round the county.'

'Stapleton!' exclaimed Harry. 'Hey, that's less than ten miles from our village!'

'Right,' said Rav. 'So within half an hour Mr Jenkins had arranged for all the members of Farm Watch to keep an eye on every bridge and crossroads within twenty miles of the unit where the pigs were stolen from. The result was they caught the rustlers red-handed just before lunchtime today.'

'So did you manage to file a report?' Siri was eager to know.

'Well, we did a nice little chat to camera with Mrs Jenkins about what's been going on,' said Ron, 'but we missed all the action.'

'What? Mum on the telly!' Wedge laughed. 'She'll be chuffed to bits!'

'But it wasn't exactly what you'd call headline stuff,' said Rav. 'Never mind. At least we finished early. So we thought we'd drop by the river and find out how you guys were getting on with the birdwatching.'

The GOGOs looked at one another, wondering which of them should break the

news that Rav and Ron had just missed yet
another really good story. And then they all
spoke at once.

'Wait! Wait!' cried Rav, trying to get the
details into his notebook. 'And you say this
guy is being questioned by the local police
right now? And that the van with all the rare
eggs in it is at the police station, too? Then
maybe it's not too late to film a story! Come
on, Ron!'

'Hey!' yelled Siri as they made a dash
for their car. 'How about an interview with
some eyewitnesses? Don't forget it was
Wedge and Harry who discovered that the
marsh harriers' eggs had been stolen from
their nest. And it was us lot who rescued the
deputy warden!'

'Good idea!' said Rav. 'We'll have to be quick but I'll get my microphone.'

Ron set up his camera. 'Now, can you all stand here by the slipway with your backs to the river?'

While Rav was interviewing Wedge, asking how he got interested in rare birds,

Harry's fingers were feeling for the cards on his key-ring. One of them, he was pleased to note, was still warm. He could feel the raised outline of Plesiosaurus under his thumb. Gently but firmly, he stroked it *nose-to-tail*.

'Show yourself!' he said under his breath. 'But not too clearly . . . You know what I mean!'

Chapter 13

Sam had slipped out to see her friend
Bekka, so she wasn't at home when Wedge
dropped Harry off at his house and crept
in behind him to say hi to her.

Mum and Nan were both very
interested to hear about their adventures.
They *ooohed* and *aaahed* about poor Mike
Lines and his broken leg and they *tut-tutted*
about the egg-thief.

The back door slammed just as Nan
was saying, 'So you think you might all

end up on the
news, do you?'

Sam had
obviously just seen
Wedge's pick-up
and she was clearly
still in a mood with
him. She stormed

into the room just as Nan added, 'It should

be on in a couple
of minutes. Shall
we turn the telly
on and have a
look?'

'What are *you*
doing here?' Sam
hissed at Wedge.

'Wedge and Harry are going to be on the news,' said Mum.

'What! What for?'

'Just sit down for a moment, dear, and you'll see.'

Sam sat down on the sofa as far away from Wedge as she could and peered at the screen. First, they had to watch ten minutes of normal, boring news. Then the newsreader started talking about a man who had been caught red-handed with hundreds of rare birds' eggs and Harry shouted, 'Here we go!'

The report started with Rav at the police station and there was a shot of all the eggs packed in the van. Then there was Rav talking to the camera.

'It turns out that the suspect carries ladders on his van everywhere he goes,' he said. 'And what's his job? He's a builder and decorator! A perfect cover for a man who needs a ladder to rob nests in high places. He also had a powerboat that he used to get to birds nesting on the marshes or on cliffs. I say he *had* a powerboat . . .' Here Rav gave a wink and a flash of the family smile. 'Because today his luck ran out when his boat exploded! Earlier I spoke to a group of young birdwatchers who were nearby when this happened.'

And there they all were . . . Wedge, Harry, Siri, Charlie and Jack. They were all looking very proud, apart from Harry, who kept glancing towards the river. Just at the

point when there was a handsome close-up
of Wedge explaining how he got interested
in kayaking and birdwatching, Sam gave a
little gasp and a squeal. She dived at Wedge
and threw her arms around him.

'Oh, come on!' said Wedge with a little
laugh. 'I ain't that good-looking!'

'I wasn't looking at you!' she croaked,

hardly able to speak. 'Well, I *was*, but there was something behind you. Didn't you see it?'

'See what?'

'Are you kidding? It was swimming in the river behind you! A huge sea-monster!'

Chapter 14

The GOGOs were all sat round the table in Siri's dining room, sipping delicious mango drinks and nibbling on crisps. Harry's sister and Wedge were there, too, and Sum had her arm round Wedge's waist. So were Siri's parents, cousin Rav *and* Rav's mum and dad. Everyone was trying to get a good view of Rav's laptop screen.

The scene where Rav had interviewed Wedge and the gang by the river had been posted on the Internet. Rav played it five

times. At first, there were shouts and showers
of crumbs as people yelled, 'There!' and,
'That is definitely the river-monster's head!'
and, 'Yes, but it could be just the movement
of the waves!' But then all the adults insisted
on no shouting, especially with mouths
full. After that, there was a lot of muffled
grunting, sudden nodding, pointing and
jumping out of seats.

'At last my boy has had some luck!' cried

Rav's mum, grabbing his face in both hands and planting a noisy kiss on his cheek. 'He lands himself in the right place at the right time and the phone has not stopped ringing!'

'It looked to me like a plesiosaurus's neck rising out of the river,' said Siri's dad, who was a professor. 'Wouldn't you agree, Harry? You're the one with the bucketful of dinosaurs, so you should know!'

'Not any more,' mumbled Harry, blushing. 'I got rid of that bucket ages ago.'

'Well, with those humps rising behind the head in the water, it looked like the Loch Ness Monster to me,' declared Siri's mum. 'But whatever it was, it was very strange and quite remarkable!'

Rav beamed with delight. 'The silly thing is, none of us saw the beast at the time. And now a lot of people are saying that we faked it. Or they say the shapes might just be waves or low trees or shadows. But the important thing is – millions of people are talking about it, and the report has got my name on it!'

'And Wedge gets a nice mention!' said Sam, giving him a squeeze and the kind of look she normally saved for

fluffy kittens or puppy dogs.

'Yes, but not us!' complained Siri.

'That's because you're too young,' explained Rav kindly. 'Sorry, but at least your friends will know who you are.'

As usual, Jack didn't say much until the gang was heading down to the park for a go on the skateboarding ramps. 'I can't believe you didn't see anything, Harry,' he said, tipping his weight back so that his BMX flipped on to its back wheel. 'You were next to the powerboat *and* you're the only one looking towards the river right before Nessie – or whatever – popped up. And yet you didn't see either the explosion *or* the sea-monster. Unlucky!'

'Yeah,' said Charlie, flipping her
dragon-skateboard to one side to avoid a
drain-cover. 'You must be really annoyed.'

Siri was puffing along on his bike, trying
to keep pace with Harry, who kept making

little spurts forward by standing on his
pedals. The same sort of questions had
crossed his mind.

'How come? Explain yourself, man!'
he demanded.

Harry knew he couldn't tell the truth. But the GOGOs would need a good reason why he hadn't seen anything. Up ahead was a thick hedge. As they got closer, he suddenly steered straight into it.

'Whoops!' Harry said as he tumbled off his bike and sent Siri's into a wild skid. 'Sorry, Siri! I didn't realize the hedge was that close!'

'That explains it!' exclaimed Siri, rubbing a bruised knee. 'You obviously need glasses!'

'I think you may be right,' said Harry, smiling.

At the same time, he was thinking: *And if you'd seen what I've seen lately, I reckon you might have your eyes tested!*

It all started with a Scarecrow.

Puffin is seventy years old.
Sounds ancient, doesn't it? But Puffin has never been
so lively. We're always on the lookout for the next big
idea, which is how it began all those years ago.

Penguin Books was a big idea from the mind of
a man called Allen Lane, who in 1935 invented
the quality paperback and changed the world.
**And from great Penguins, great Puffins grew,
changing the face of children's books forever.**

The first four Puffin Picture Books were hatched in 1940 and the
first Puffin story book featured a man with broomstick arms called
Worzel Gummidge. In 1967 Kaye Webb, Puffin Editor, started the
Puffin Club, promising to **'make children into readers'**.
She kept that promise and over 200,000 children became
devoted Puffineers through their quarterly instalments of
Puffin Post, which is now back for a new generation.

Many years from now, we hope you'll look back and
remember Puffin with a smile. **No matter what your age
or what you're into, there's a Puffin for everyone.**
The possibilities are endless, but one thing is for sure:
whether it's a picture book or a paperback, a sticker book
or a hardback, **if it's got that little Puffin
on it – it's bound to be good.**